LOST

IN THE **DESERT** OF **DREAD**

WARNING!

The instructions in this book are for extreme survival
situations only. Always proceed with caution, and ask
an adult to supervise – or, ideally, seek professional
help. If in doubt, consult a responsible adult.

Published 2014 by
A & C Black, an imprint of
Bloomsbury Publishing Plc
50 Bedford Square, London, WC1B 3DP

www.bloomsbury.com

ISBN 978-1-4081-9466-9

A CIP catalogue for this book is available from the British Library.

Printed by CPI Group (UK) Ltd, Croydon CR0 4YY

1 3 5 7 9 10 8 6 4 2

MIX
Paper from
responsible sources
FSC® C020471

LOST

IN THE **DESERT** OF **DREAD**

TRACEY TURNER

A & C BLACK
AN IMPRINT OF BLOOMSBURY
LONDON NEW DELHI NEW YORK SYDNEY

Africa

Mediterranean Sea

Morocco
Tunisia
Algeria
Libya
Egypt
Western Sahara
Red Sea
Sahara Desert
Mauritania
Mali
Niger
Chad
Sudan
Eritrea
Senegal
Guinea
Burkina Faso
Nigeria
South Sudan
Ethiopia
Sierra Leone
Ivory Coast
Ghana
Benin
Togo
Central African Republic
Liberia
Cameroon
Somalia
Gulf of Guinea
Gabon
Congo
DR Congo
Uganda
Kenya
ATLANTIC OCEAN
Angola
Tanzania
INDIAN OCEAN
Zambia
Malawi
Mozambique
Madagascar
Namibia
Zimbabwe
Botswana
South Africa

Welcome to your adventure!
STOP! Read this first!

Welcome to an action-packed adventure in which you take the starring role!

You're about to enter the Sahara Desert, one of the most inhospitable places on Earth. On each page choose from different options – according to your instincts, knowledge and intelligence – and make your own path through the desert to safety.

You decide . . .
- How to escape a deadly scorpion
- Where to find water in a parched desert landscape
- How to handle a pack of hungry hyenas

. . . and many more life-or-death dilemmas. Along the way you'll discover the facts you need to help you survive.

It's time to test your survival skills – or die trying!

Your adventure starts on page 7.

You open your eyes and blink quickly to get rid of the sand. You're lying on the desert floor with your backpack next to you, completely covered by a blanket.

It's swelteringly hot. You throw the blanket off, and with it a thick layer of fine sand, which also seems to have found its way into your hair, nose, eyes and clothes. The sun is so dazzling that you have to shield your eyes. You look around you – the arid desert landscape stretches for as far as you can see in every direction.

You piece together the events that led you here: you were on a camel safari, part of a group of ten people, including two knowledgeable guides. A sandstorm blew up: the noise of the howling wind, and the sand flying in all directions was confusing and disorienting. You thought you were following everyone else, but you must have been stumbling blindly in the wrong direction. There's a movement in the bright blue sky – a dark shape circles. You gulp: it's a vulture.

There is no one to be seen. The sun beats down relentlessly. You are completely lost, and, as far as you can tell, totally alone. You know you need to find help. But where?

You set off with nothing but the clothes on your back and your backpack, which contains a few useful things that might help you in your journey.

How will you survive?

Turn to page 8 to find information you need to help you survive.

The Sahara Desert is the largest hot desert in the world. It stretches for more than nine million square kilometres across most of the northern part of Africa, in the countries Algeria, Chad, Egypt, Libya, Mali, Mauritania, Morocco, Niger, Western Sahara, Sudan and Tunisia, from the Atlantic Ocean in the west to the Red Sea in the east. It's one of the hottest places on Earth, and one of the most hostile. People have walked into the vast, scorching desert never to return. If you're going to survive you'll need to have your wits about you.

Desert Perils

The desert's lack of water is the greatest peril for any traveller – find out more on page 49 and 81. Danger also lurks in the form of deadly scorpions and snakes: the deathstalker scorpion is one of the most deadly on earth; the saw-scaled viper is responsible for thousands of human deaths every year. There are also larger animals that might prove to be a threat: baboons, ostriches, hyenas and jackals.

Saharan Landscape

Think of the Sahara and you probably imagine enormous dunes of fine, shifting sand. Sand dunes like this, known as ergs, can rise up to 180 metres high, and take up about 20% of the Sahara Desert. Most of the desert is made up of dry, rocky plains, called regs. Hamadas are large areas of exposed rock, which have been worn smooth by the wind. There are mountains in the Sahara too – the highest peak reaches more than 3400 metres high. Apart from the Nile River, there are no permanent rivers or streams in the Sahara. Known as wadis, rivers or streams are seasonal and most of the time they're dry. Water reaches the surface at oases.

Desert Life

It might look like a lifeless wasteland, but some plants and animals thrive in the hot, dry conditions of the Sahara. Plants include the baobab and acacia trees, grasses and shrubs. Some have long roots that reach underground water reserves – especially those near wadis or oases, such as date palms. Animals include jerboas (small rodents), addax (a type of antelope), Barbary sheep, camels (which were introduced to the Sahara around AD 200), as well as deadly scorpions, spiders, ants and venomous snakes. Most people who live in the Sahara live near the oases. There are also nomads, who herd animals and trade between oases and cities on the fringes of the desert.

Dry Desert

Deserts are defined by their lack of rainfall: they receive less than 250 millimetres of rain per year. In the Sahara, most regions receive less than 130 millimetres of rain on average, though in the mountains it rains more. Rainfall is very variable – some areas might have no rain at all for a number of years, then 500 millimetres might fall in a sudden downpour.

Sizzling Sun

During the day the Sahara is hot. Temperatures of around 38 degrees Celsius are common, but it can reach to more than 50 degrees Celsius. The highest temperature ever recorded in the Sahara was a blistering 58 degrees Celsius! At night, the temperature plummets, often by 25 degrees or even more. During the winter months the temperature often falls below freezing at night.

Turn to page 10.

Desert Survival Tips

Here are a few basic tips that might affect your chances of survival in the desert . . .

- Water is your first priority and you need to be aware of how much you need. This varies dramatically according to temperature and whether or not you are using energy, but you might be surprised at how much water you need in hot conditions. Someone working strenuously in 40 degree heat would need 20 litres of water a day! However it can also be very dangerous to consume too much water. There's a chart on page 119 to show water consumption.

- Keep your skin covered – it will burn very easily if you don't. Loose clothing will help keep you cooler as you sweat (the wet cloth against your skin will cool you down). Cover your head, too – if you don't you risk getting heat stroke.

- Keeping hydrated isn't enough, you need salt too because you lose salt as you sweat.

- Don't eat – it will only make you thirstier.

- Breathe through your nose to conserve as much moisture as possible.

- The temperature drops dramatically at night so make sure you have something warm to wrap up in.

- If you have no idea at all where you are, you are probably better off staying in one place, signalling as best you can, and awaiting rescue. But where's the fun in that?

Even though the sun isn't at its highest point in the sky, it is still blisteringly hot. You dread to think what the temperature will be like at midday, as you stagger across the barren, rocky ground towards the meagre shade offered by a large boulder. You sit down while you decide what to do.

You could stay put and wait for rescue – maybe you could spell out SOS with rocks. On the other hand, you could easily die of thirst before help arrives. You think about it . . . you feel you have to do something – just sitting around waiting will drive you mad.

You check in your backpack – things could be a lot worse. You were one of the water carriers in your group and so you have four litres of water in plastic bottles. You take a grateful swig from one of them. There are matches in your backpack too which will come in handy for making fires, as well as several other useful items including a spade, sun cream and an aluminium mess tin, which you can use to boil water. You're well dressed for the desert in a loose cotton shirt, trousers and a scarf which you can wrap around your face in case of another sand storm. You also have a blanket for the cold night.

The water you have probably won't last very long if you walk in this terrible heat, so you'll have to find another water source pretty quickly. It will last much longer if you rest and travel at night, though.

If you decide to go in search of water, turn to page 26.

If you decide to rest now, shelter from the sun, and travel later, turn to page 22.

You feel as though you're being slowly roasted. The trees seem much farther away than you thought. It can be hard to judge distances in the desert, because there aren't any of the objects you'd normally use for reference – cars, lamp posts, people. A pile of rocks could be small and quite close, or large and far away. The same goes for trees, if you're not familiar with the type. You're sweating so much that your cotton shirt is drenched, and the weighty backpack feels heavier than ever. Maybe if you took off some of your clothes you might feel a bit cooler?

If you decide to take off some clothes, go to page 16

If you decide to carry on as you are, go to page 35.

You wriggle out of the cave. You're right to be careful of dark, enclosed spaces – there could be snakes or other creatures lurking in there. And, in fact, in that cave there were deadly scorpions!

You make yourself comfortable in the shade. Even though you're still hot, resting and keeping as cool as you can is the best policy in the desert during the day. At night the temperature drops dramatically and the exercise will keep you warm. You rest and doze, making sure you take sips of water whenever you're awake.

As dusk begins to fall, you spot a dry stream bed and decide to go and investigate, in search of water.

Go to page 28.

You approach the feeding pack. Most of the jackals scatter, but three remain, feeding on the animal carcass – it looks like a young gazelle. The meat looks fresh, and isn't smelly, so it must be a recent kill. The jackals seem to be nervous creatures, and you're not worried. You think about using some of your matches to get a fire going and roasting some of the meat.

You're a metre or so from the dead animal. Two of the jackals lope off, but the remaining one growls at you and bares its teeth. You wave your arms, expecting it to run away, but it runs towards you. You aim a kick, miss, and the jackal bites your arm. You cry out in pain. The wound isn't bleeding much, but it's very painful. You aim another kick at the jackal and it runs off to join the rest of its pack.

You sit down, feeling faint. You know that all members of the dog family harbour a wide variety of bacteria in their mouths, so you use some of your water to wash the wound. The bleeding soon stops, but unfortunately, despite the fact that you poured water on the wound, the jackal has given you blood poisoning, also known as sepsis. Soon the wound is red, painful and oozing pus. You feel weak and dizzy, and have to lie down. Alone and without medical attention, you're too weak to find more water. The infection and lack of water soon kill you.

The end.

Jackals

- There are three species of African jackal: the common or golden jackal, the side-striped jackal, and the black-backed jackal. The golden jackal is the one that lives in northern Africa, and it's also the biggest, at about one metre long and half a metre to the shoulder.

- Jackals usually hunt singly or in pairs, although sometimes bigger family groups hunt in packs. Groups might congregate to feed on carrion.

- Jackals eat a wide variety of food: they prey on rodents, small mammals, lizards, snakes, carrion, fruit, insects (including dungbeetles) and also young gazelles. They attack animals up to three times their own weight. However, it's extremely unusual for them to attack a human being – usually they will run away.

- Jackals are crepuscular (active at dawn and dusk), to avoid the heat of the desert sun.

You take off your shirt and trousers, but you don't feel any better, and soon you put your clothes back on, realising that you were cooler before anyway. The skin across your shoulders stings as you put your shirt on.

By the time you get to the parched-looking trees, you're sunburnt, exhausted and dehydrated. There's no visible water. Wearily, you begin to dig – but this just makes you sweat even more and you soon develop heat exhaustion and then heat stroke. You crawl into a patch of shade under a tree. Your last thought is that you should have rested until nightfall.

The end.

→ Heat Stroke

- Heat exhaustion occurs when the body temperature rises above 37 degrees Celsius, which can be treated by drinking water and keeping cool.

- Heat stroke occurs when the body temperature is above 40 degrees Celsius. Victims can be confused, with shallow and quick breathing.

- If heat stroke isn't treated immediately, the body overheats and organs stop functioning normally, eventually leading to death.

You're pretty sure this is south. Ahead of you stretches a gravelly, arid plain, with dunes in the distance. It doesn't look very promising. But you trudge off, using the dunes and a rocky escarpment to your right to keep you on your course.

Go to page 50.

Unknown to you, there are scorpions in this shallow cave, sheltering from the heat of the day just as you are. One, a large deathstalker, is scuttling further back into the cave to get away from you when you move your foot and kick it by accident. Alarmed, the scorpion raises its deadly sting and strikes, injecting a lethal dose of venom into your ankle.

The pain from the sting is agonising. You curse yourself for not checking inside first as you hurriedly move out of the cave to avoid risking another sting. You don't know what's stung you, but you remember there are dangerous scorpions in the Sahara.

Your ankle becomes numb. You use some water to wash it, in case it helps. Unfortunately, it doesn't. Your tongue becomes swollen, you feel dizzy and feverish, and begin to have difficulty swallowing and breathing. Your heart races.

It's not long before the scorpion's venom kills you.

The end.

Deathstalker Scorpion

- The deathstalker scorpion is one of the world's most venomous scorpions. Despite this, a sting from a deathstalker wouldn't usually kill a healthy adult human – though the sting is extremely painful. If you are sick, a child or an old person, you're in more danger.

- Deathstalkers are found in North Africa and the Middle East. They can grow up to about ten centimetres long and are yellowish in colour.

- They prey on insects and spiders. Their pincers are weak, which is why their venom is so powerful – so that it kills prey quickly to stop it scuttling out of the scorpion's grasp.

- Along with most other scorpions, deathstalkers are nocturnal, spending the day in burrows or under rocks.

- There are more than 1,500 different species of scorpion. Most live in desert regions, but there are also scorpions that live in rainforests and temperate regions.

- In times of food shortage, scorpions are able to lower their metabolic rate so that they can survive long periods – up to a year – without eating.

- Scorpions usually prey on insects and other invertebrates, but they'll eat almost anything, including other scorpions.

A movement catches your eye: in the moonlight you spot a snake side-winding down a sand dune, leaving a regular pattern behind it. It's a sand viper, which prey mostly on lizards. You watch as it moves gracefully off on its night time hunt.

The dunes stretch into the distance, where they look as though they must be several storeys high.

Should you trek along the sand dune, or find another route? It'll mean changing from your chosen course.

If you decide to alter your course away from the sand dune, turn to page 50.

If you decide to walk in the dune, turn to page 44.

The building's little more than a tiny mud hut, half falling down, but it provides all the shade you need. After checking for creatures, you spread out your blanket and rest all day in the heat, making sure you drink enough water. As dusk descends and the temperature rapidly cools, you pick up your things and decide which direction to take.

But your attention's caught by some noises outside. You investigate, and discover a group of what look like dogs in the distance. You recognise them as jackals. It looks as though they've found a dead animal to eat.

As long as the animal is recently dead, you could shoo away the jackals, then make a fire and cook some of the meat for yourself.

If you decide to shoo away the jackals from their food, go to page 14.

If you decide to steer clear of the animals, go to page 36.

You scan the landscape for somewhere suitable to shelter from the sun for the day. There's a ridge of higher ground with plenty of big boulders that should provide shade. Or, further away, you can see what looks like a small rectangular building.

If you decide to head for the building, go to page 21

If you decide to shelter amongst the rocks, go to page 51.

Shelter in the Desert

- When you're sheltering in the daytime in the desert, your first priority is shade. You can find natural shade in rocky areas, and you might even find deserted buildings. You could also use a bush for shelter with a blanket (or other covering) thrown over it.

- Shelters below-ground can reduce the desert heat considerably, but first consider the amount of effort needed, and whether it's worth it. If it's already hot, don't bother digging a shelter as you'll use up too much water by sweating.

- If it's not too hot yet, you could try digging a trench about 50 centimetres deep and long and wide enough for you to lie down in comfortably. Pile earth or sand from your trench around three sides, leaving the fourth side open for you to enter and exit the shelter. Secure your blanket or other covering over the top. Ideally, the outer covering should be white to reflect the heat, and you should have a second layer underneath it, with an air pocket in between.

- If you're sheltering at night in the desert, you need to keep as warm as possible – make sure there's something underneath you and don't lie on the cold ground. Don't make your shelter in a valley bottom, which will be especially cold and prone to frost.

- Wherever you're sheltering in the desert, make sure it's free from insects and reptiles that might give you a nasty bite or sting.

- Always avoid areas that could flood in a sudden downpour, such as dry river beds – however unlikely it seems, flash floods do happen in deserts.

Deciding to carry on even though the temperature is above 30 degrees Celsius, and the sun is now burning any exposed skin on your body, was not a good idea. Even though you've been drinking lots of water, your body has been sweating heavily, getting rid of salt as a result.

The very low salt levels in your body have led to hyponatraemia. Your body is unable to process water, making the cells in your body expand. As the cells in your brain expand, you feel dizzy and confused. It's not long before you're forced to lie down. You fall into a coma and die.

The end.

Hyponatraemia

- We need salt to live. Hyponatraemia is a low level of salt in the blood.

- It can be caused by drinking too much water (yes, even water can be bad for you) – for example if you're working out at the gym and drinking lots but not replacing the salt that you've lost as you sweat, or if you lose a lot of body fluids (caused by severe diarrhoea or vomiting). Hyponatraemia can also be caused by kidney failure and heart failure, and some other conditions.

- When salt is low, the body's cells swell up with water. When brain cells swell it's especially dangerous because the skull limits how much the brain can expand, causing it to press on the skull.

- Symptoms of hyponatraemia include headache, confusion, tiredness, nausea, muscle spasms and seizures.

- In severe cases, hyponatraemia can be fatal.

You gaze across the barren landscape and a smudge of green catches your eye. In the distance you can make out a clump of trees – that must mean water.

You put on sunglasses, make a head covering out of a spare white shirt in your backpack, and set off. The bottles of water in your backpack are heavy and almost straight away your back is soaked through with sweat.

Crossing the gravelly, dry plain towards the trees you are baking hot, but you're convinced that finding water should be your top priority in the desert.

Go to page 12.

Adapting for the Desert

As a human being, you're not particularly well equipped for desert survival. Desert plants and animals have adapted to cope with the hot, dry conditions . . .

- Most desert animals are nocturnal, taking advantage of the cool of the night. They spend the hot days resting, many of them in underground burrows.

- Some animals don't need to drink water at all – they get the moisture they need from the plants or animals they eat. The addax, for example, a large Saharan antelope, gets water from sucking plants.

- Many desert animals conserve water by not sweating, and only passing small amounts of concentrated urine.

- Some animals cool down by peeing on their legs! Turkey vultures do this.

- Because fat increases body heat, some animals have adapted by concentrating their body fat in one place, such as in a hump (like camels) or at the base of the animal's tail (like some lizards).

- Some desert plants store water in their roots, stems, leaves or fruit. The baobab tree, for example, stores water in its trunk – it gets fatter and thinner at different times of year, depending on how much water it's storing.

- Desert plants' leaves might be glossy, to reflect the sun, and/or waxy, to keep in moisture.

- Some desert plants have very long roots that reach down to underground water supplies. Others have shallow roots, taking advantage of surface water.

As you get to the pile of stones in the gloomy dusk light, you're even more convinced that they have been placed there deliberately. You move them and, sure enough, they're covering a water hole.

You take some water in your cupped hands – it looks and smells clean. Should you bother to make a fire and boil it? It would be time-consuming, and it's difficult to see what might have contaminated it.

If you decide to make a fire and boil the water, go to page 45.

If you decide not to bother boiling the water and fill up your containers and carry on, go to page 46.

Making a Fire in the Desert

- Dry desert conditions are perfect for making a fire. The main problem, especially here in the Sahara, is fuel. You need tinder (flammable material such as wood shavings), kindling (small twigs) and fuel (larger pieces of wood for when the fire is burning well). Gather any wood you see in the Sahara. If you can't find any wood, you could try dried animal droppings!

- Choose a sheltered spot for your fire, where the wind won't blow it out, and make sure it's not too near a tree or other plants that could catch fire. If the wind is very strong you might need to dig a trench to make your fire. Put a circle of rocks around it to conserve the heat and fuel.

- Make a bed of tinder (this could be dry grass) and make a wigwam of kindling around it. Light the tinder with a match. Only start adding larger pieces of wood when the kindling is burning well.

- Luckily you have some matches with you, but if you didn't you would have to try creating a spark to light your tinder using friction. At its most basic this could be rubbing two sticks together, but a fire plough is a more sophisticated method: cut a groove in a flat piece of wood, then rub a sharpened stick up and down it (the stick will need to be harder wood than the flat piece). This will create shavings that act as tinder, which will catch alight from a spark.

- During the day, you could ignite kindling by directing the sun's rays through a lens or the bottom of a glass bottle.

You sit down in a small patch of shade and scan the landscape for somewhere to rest. You take a drink, and rummage at the bottom of your backpack for a sachet of salt, which you sprinkle into the bottle – you've been sweating so much that you probably need it.

In the distance you spot what looks like a small rectangular building – it might be a good place to rest for the day. As the sun beats down, you can see that it was foolish to try and walk in the desert during the day, when it's burning hot. It's much better to rest now, then set off in search of rescue when the temperature drops at dusk.

Go to page 21.

It's dark inside the small cave, soothing your eyes, which ache from the brightness of the sun. It's cooler, too – you've got a much better chance of comfortable rest here. You move a few small rocks and pebbles, and put the blanket underneath you to make a soft bed.

You hear scuttling. There are probably other animals in here that are sheltering from the heat too. Should you move from your comfortable position?

If you decide to move, go to page 13.

If you decide to stay where you are, go to page 18.

The snake is a saw-scaled viper, one of the most venomous and aggressive snakes in Africa. This one was out hunting when you got too close. Its body looped into S shapes, the snake rubs its scales together, which makes a warning hissing noise. Because you haven't backed off, it strikes, lightning fast.

The snake has bitten your ankle. You stagger backwards, away from the snake, in agonising pain. The bite starts to swell. Soon you feel feverish and vomit. You need anti-venom and hospital care, but alone in the middle of the desert you're not going to get it. The snake's venom stops blood from clotting and leads to kidney failure.

The end.

Saw-scaled Viper

- There are eight species of saw-scaled viper, which live north of the equator across Africa, Arabia, and southwestern Asia, including India and Sri Lanka.

- They're between about 30 centimetres and one metre long, with a thick body, and can be brown, grey or orange with darker spots and blotches. They have serrated scales, which make the hissing noise you heard. They use it as a warning, like a rattlesnake's rattle.

- The snakes are nocturnal, feeding on small mammals, birds, lizards, scorpions and other invertebrates.

- Saw-scaled vipers are extremely aggressive, and their venom is very powerful.

- There are snakes with more powerful venom, but where saw-scaled vipers are found, they're responsible for more human deaths than all other snakes in the region put together.

- The snakes cause thousands of deaths per year – as well as unpopulated areas of the Sahara, they also live in close proximity to people.

You set off again. It's chilly, and you're glad of the blanket around your shoulders.

You spot a movement from the corner of your eye: there are some rocks just beside you, and you thought you saw something climbing them. You investigate . . . and come face to face with a gorgeous, fluffy cat. It has big ears and a very cute face and it's looking at you in surprise.

You're not sure if it's some kind of wild desert cat, or whether it's a domestic cat – in which case there must be people nearby. Should you stroke it, and let it lead you to where it lives?

If you decide to approach the cat, go to page 58.

If you decide to leave it alone, go to page 54.

You've never felt so hot. Sweat drenches your clothes and trickles down the sides of your face as you walk. Something glints in the sunlight. To your horror, you see it's the bleached bones of a large dead animal, its ribs pointing towards the sky.

A shiver runs down your spine despite the extreme heat. You're feeling a bit dizzy, too – maybe it's the sight of the animal skeleton.

Perhaps it's time to admit defeat and find shelter from the sun, then walk at night instead.

If you decide to seek shelter, go to page 30.

If you decide to keep going, go to page 24.

The sun is beginning to slip below the horizon, so you can now work out which way is north, south, east and west. You are sure you don't want to go north – when you set off for your desert trek you were at the southern edge of the desert. You reckon the direction you should take is south or southwest of where you are now.

You point the number twelve on your watch face in the direction of the sun . . . which way should you go?

If you decide to follow the direction of the number 6, go to page 20.

If you decide to follow the number 9, go to page 17.

If you decide to follow the number 10, go to page 48.

Using a Watch as a Compass

Even if the sun isn't conveniently setting or rising, you can work out which way is north, south, east and west using a watch with hands.

- With the watch in the palm of your hand, point the hour hand towards the sun (but don't look at the sun or you could damage your eyes).

- In the northern hemisphere, the sun is due south at midday. That means you can work out which way is south by dividing the angle between the hour hand (which is the position of the sun now) and the twelve on the watch face. So if it was two o'clock in the afternoon, the one on the watch face would point south.

- If you only have a digital watch, just draw a clock face in the sand with the hour hand pointing at the sun.

- If you don't know what the time is, stand a stick in the sand and measure its shadow at different times of day. In the northern hemisphere, the shortest shadow will point north.

- At night, you can find north if you know which star is Polaris, the North Star.

You pause for a moment, a bit puffed out, and look back to a rock next to a withered tree you noticed just after you set off. It's a long way away now – you've covered a lot of ground.

Even though the night is cold, you're very warm, tired from carrying your heavy backpack, and sweating. Maybe you should slow down?

If you decide to slow down go to page 74.

If you carry on jogging and walking, go to page 80.

It's dusk, and the temperature's already dropping dramatically. The sun's slipping over the horizon quickly – the twilight doesn't last for long this close to the equator. You get up and shake out your blanket. Soon it will be cold enough to wrap it around you as you walk.

Not far away from you there's a wadi – a dry river bed. There's a pile of stones in it, and the stones look as though they might have been deliberately placed on top of one another. Should you go and find out what it is, or is it better to make a decision about which direction you need to head in, before you do anything else?

If you decide to work out your direction first, go to page 36.

If you decide to investigate the stones in the wadi, go to page 28.

As you get closer to the high ground, you realise there are more hyenas than you thought – they seem to be everywhere. They're bigger than you thought, too. Still, you reason, hyenas are cowardly scavengers. And anyway, who could be frightened of an animal that laughs?

You should be frightened, though, because hyenas are dangerous animals that have been known to attack and kill people. A few of them lope towards you, spreading out to your right and left. You're worried now – but it's too late. Two of the hyenas run at you and attack. At least it's all over pretty quickly.

The end.

Spotted Hyenas

- There are four types of hyena – brown, striped, aardwolf and spotted. Spotted hyenas are the largest species – they are huge, measuring up to about 1.5 metres long, and up to about 80 kilograms in weight! They live mainly in sub-Saharan Africa.

- They don't just scavenge food – hyenas are skilled pack hunters that prey on animals as large as wildebeest.

- Spotted hyenas make a variety of noises to communicate with one another, including their famous 'laugh'.

- They live together in large groups of up to about 100 animals. Female hyenas, which are larger than males, lead the group.

- Despite their appearance, hyenas are more closely related to cats than dogs.

- Hyenas' jaws are extremely powerful – capable of crunching bones – and they can even digest teeth, so that nothing goes to waste.

- Hyenas do attack and kill people, sometimes even dragging people from their beds at night.

You shelter at the base of the dune as the wind howls even louder and sand and grit whirl through the air in choking clouds. Soon it's impossible to see anything in the swirling sandstorm. You cover up exposed skin because when the sandy wind touches your bare skin it feels like sandpaper.

Unfortunately, you've picked the wrong place to shelter. Unless there's thunder and lightning, when you could run the risk of a lightning strike, it's better to head for higher ground in a sandstorm, because the sand, grit and dust is denser the lower down you are. And a sand dune was an especially bad place to pick – since it is made entirely of sand! Lorry loads of it are picked up and dumped down again, totally burying you underneath a thick, suffocating layer.

The end.

Sandstorms

- Sandstorms are caused by strong winds blowing over loose sand or earth. Most are small and only last a matter of minutes – but the biggest can be more than a kilometre high, hundreds of kilometres wide, and travel at 120 kilometres per hour.

- It's very easy to become lost in a sandstorm (that's how you ended up lost in the desert in the first place), because the whirling sand makes it impossible to see. It's best not to move about, since it's easy to become disoriented.

- The best thing to do is find shelter (though not by a sand dune), cover your nose and mouth with cloth, and wrap the rest of your body in whatever you have to hand to stop the sand and grit from hurting your skin. Then wait the sandstorm out.

Walking on the sand dune is a bit like walking through treacle – your feet sink deep into the sand, and every step takes a huge effort. Despite the cold, you're starting to sweat. The dune is enormous, and stretches away into the distance in the bright moonlight. Maybe you should find easier terrain.

If you decide to turn back, altering your course, go to page 50.

If you decide to carry on walking on the dune, go to page 64.

You're almost optimistic about your situation now that you've got plenty of water. You're feeling pretty fit, the moon's bright enough to see by, and you're not too cold as long as you keep moving.

The desert looks endless – mile after mile of scrubby, almost featureless rocky landscape. The desert's so big, it could take a long time to find help. You remember hearing that the most efficient way to cover ground is to jog for a few paces, then walk for a few paces – this is how soldiers cover ground quickly. Maybe you should do the same.

If you decide to jog and walk, go to page 38.

If you decide to walk go to page 74.

Did you really think it was a good idea not to bother boiling the water? Oh dear.

You don't realise it for a few days, but you've contracted amoebic dysentery from the water, which gives you bad diarrhoea, vomiting, pain and fever. The diarrhoea on its own is enough to kill you, since you're unable to replace the lost fluids and salts, but even if you weren't you would need medical care in order to recover.

The end.

Dysentery

- There are two types of dysentery, one caused by bacteria and the other caused by amoebae, single-celled parasites that live in your intestine.

- Both types of dysentery can be passed on through poor hygiene, or by consuming contaminated food or water. In some people, amoebic dysentery can be life-threatening.

- Symptoms of amoebic dysentery include diarrhoea, stomach pain, vomiting and fever.

- Amoebic dysentery can be treated with drugs. If not, it can be fatal.

The bite is so painful it feels as though it's throbbing, and the scratches are sore too. You decide to take a chance by using some of your valuable water. First you take a long swig, then you use some of the water to wash the wounds. The small holes where the cat's teeth punctured your skin are very painful to the touch, but you reason that washing them can't possibly do any harm. You know you don't have any soap, but you rummage around in your backpack for something that might help. To your surprise and relief, you discover a tube of antiseptic cream. You apply the cream, and wrap a spare cotton scarf around the bite and the scratches. Before long, you're feeling much better.

Now you need to find more water to replenish the water you used to wash your wounds.

Go to page 64.

You set off on your course, just to the left of the setting sun. The temperature's dropping fast. Before long, you spot something that looks like a building, and hurry towards it.

As you get closer, you can see that the small adobe building's long since abandoned – half of it's in ruins. You investigate and discover a low circular wall with a heavy wooden cover on it. You can hardly believe your eyes – could this actually be a well? You take off the cover and peer down – the reflection of the bright moon glints at the bottom! There's a rope with a plastic bucket to drop down. It plops into the water with a satisfying splash and you bring up some water – the bucket leaks a bit, but it works. You drink some water and fill up your bottles.

It occurs to you that you could stay here and await rescue. On the other hand, it doesn't look as though anyone's been here for a very long time.

If you decide to stay here and await rescue, go to page 63

If you decide to move on with your full water bottles, go to page 34.

Desert Wells and Water Holes

- If you find a well or water hole in the desert, make sure you replace the cover quickly to prevent evaporation or contamination.

- You might find an animal water hole in the desert, but be careful, as the water could be contaminated with animal poo and other bacteria. One option is to dig another hole close to the water hole, so that the water filters through the sand and gravel and removes some of the impurities, then boil the water.

- The nomadic people of the Sahara know exactly where the water holes are so that they can replenish their water supplies as they move about the desert. They have to be precise – just a few kilometres in the wrong direction could spell disaster.

- If you spot flies, mosquitoes, or bees, it's a sign that water isn't far away.

- Birds can point the way to desert water sources: watch the direction of their flight in the evenings.

Suddenly you hear a sound that sends a shiver down your spine – a rasping, hissing sound. You stop dead in your tracks. You look down, to where you think the noise is coming from, but at first you can't see anything on the sandy, pebbly ground. Then you spot it. It's a snake, making its body into S-shaped loops that it slides against one another, making the rasping sound. And you're almost standing on it.

It's just a small snake – it's probably more frightened of you than you are of it. And you know that most snakes aren't venomous. Should you just ignore it? Or should you back away and run?

If you decide to step around the snake, go to page 32.

If you decide to run away, go to page 62.

The rocks offer shade from the fierce sun – they're tall, and there are enough of them that you can rest in the shade without having to move when the sun shifts across the sky. Although you're still baking hot, you no longer feel as though you're being roasted over a spit. You spread your blanket out on the ground and lie down, feeling better by the minute.

You're just about to close your eyes when you notice that there's a small, dark cave in the rocks. The entrance is big enough for you to crawl into, but not much bigger than that. It would be even cooler in there, where the sun hasn't warmed up the sand.

If you decide to crawl into the cave, go to page 31.

If you decide to rest where you are in the shade of the rocks, go to page 39.

Off to your right, you spot movement: it's a small herd of antelope, heading away from you. Maybe they've been drinking at a water hole?

You follow them and find that they've finished their drink – the moonlight glints on a small pool of water that the antelope must have just visited. Because the water hole is used by animals, you decide to be on the safe side: you dig a hole a few metres from the pool and wait for water to seep into it, that way it's filtered by the sand. While you're waiting, you make a fire (see page 29) and boil the water. It takes a while, but eventually you fill up all your bottles. At least you can be fairly sure the water isn't going to make you sick.

Go to page 84.

Cats have bacteria-ridden mouths, and a very nasty infection has started in your wrist where the sand cat bit you. The wound is inflamed, painful and oozing with pus. You pour some of your water on it, but by this time the infection has taken hold.

The wrist is an especially bad place to be bitten because it's full of blood vessels and tendons, so an infection can be spread around the body to vital organs very quickly. You start to feel weak and sick, and realise you won't be able to continue walking. Eventually, you stop by some rocks – you can see that there should be shade here in the daytime. There's no water source nearby, but the infection kills you before you run out anyway.

The end.

On the ground in front of you there's a vine-like plant bearing fruit that look like small melons – roughly about the size of oranges. Melons are famous for being juicy. They would help keep you hydrated and give you some energy for walking at the same time. On the other hand, although the fruit look like melons, you're not absolutely sure what they are – they could even be poisonous.

If you decide to eat the fruit, go to page 68.

If you decide not to, go to page 50.

Edible Desert Plants

- The African baobab tree stores drinkable water in its trunk, and the pulp in its fruit is tasty and nutritious. The trees can be 25 metres tall and live for three thousand years. They're known as upside-down trees because the branches look like roots.

- The fruit of the wild desert gourd (see page 68) can't be eaten, but the seeds can and the shoots can be chewed to obtain water.

- The Topnaar tribe of the Namib depend on the !Nara plant. Its tasty fruit is harvested once a year, and its seeds are dried and eaten as a delicacy.

- In the deserts of North America, cacti can be sources of food and water. The pulp of the fishhook barrel cactus can be squeezed to obtain water (although the water can taste horrible!), and its fruits and flesh are edible.

- The agave (also from North America) collects rainwater at the base of the plant, and some moisture is stored in its leaves and stalk.

You should have removed the tick because, unfortunately, it has passed on bacteria via its bite. You don't get any symptoms for a while, but then you start to feel feverish, with a terrible headache, and muscle and joint pain all over your body.

You have relapsing fever, which needs to be treated with antibiotics. The disease wouldn't normally kill a healthy person, but it makes you feel so ill that you aren't capable of finding water.

The end.

Parasite-borne Diseases

- Relapsing fever can be caused by ticks or lice, and both types are common in Africa. Symptoms wouldn't usually appear for at least five days. If the disease is passed on by lice it's worse, and you might die if you don't take antibiotics (even if victims are treated, one in a hundred will die anyway). Epidemics of louse-borne relapsing fever sometimes happen where living conditions are poor.

- Malaria is caused by the plasmodium parasite, which gets into the blood via the bite of a female anopheles mosquito. Symptoms appear around ten days after the bite, but they can take up to a year to appear. Over a million people die from malaria every year, mostly in Africa, because they aren't treated in time.

- Tsetse fly bites can pass on a disease known as sleeping sickness, caused by a parasite that infects the flies. There are two types of sleeping sickness – if you get the acute form, you will almost certainly die without treatment.

You approach the cat with your hand outstretched. Its eyes widen. Suddenly it flattens its large ears to its head and hisses at you, baring its pointed teeth. You remove your hand quickly, and you're just about to run away when the cat launches itself at you and sinks its teeth into your wrist, scratching your arms with its claws at the same time.

You manage to fling it off and the cat pelts away into the night.

If you decide to return to the well and the ruins for water to wash your wounds, go to page 73.

If you decide to wrap a bandage around the wound and keep going, go to page 61.

Sand Cats

- Sand cats are the only type of cat that live in deserts. They're found in both stony and sandy deserts in northern Africa and southwest and central Asia.

- They are sandy coloured, sometimes with stripes on their fur, with a ringed tail with a dark tip. They can measure up to 60 centimetres long, including the tail.

- The cats are able to survive without water, getting the moisture they need from their food, though they will drink if they find water.

- Sand cats eat small mammals, such as jerboas, gerbils, lizards and insects. They sometimes dig out their prey from underground.

- They live in burrows, where they stay during the day during the hottest months, only coming out to hunt at dusk and during the night.

As you walk on, you become aware of an uncomfortable spot on your leg. Eventually you stop and have a look at it – to your horror, you see that it's alive!

The creature is a tick, a small parasite that feeds on the blood of mammals. This one has decided to have a snack at your expense.

You have no idea whether ticks can do any harm – after all they're very small – but you do know that leeches will attach themselves to people and drink their blood without doing any harm at all. Maybe, like leeches, the tick will just drop off when it's had enough. Or maybe you should try and remove it?

If you decide to ignore the tick, go to page 56.

If you decide to remove it, go to page 89.

The pain in your arm makes you stop and examine your wounds. The scratches aren't deep, but the bite on your wrist looks red and angry, and your hand is beginning to swell.

Should you just keep going, or is it better to find water, wash the wound, and have a rest?

If you decide to keep going, go to page 53.

If you decide to stop and treat the wound, go to page 47.

You round the summit of a low hill and a wonderful sight is waiting for you on the other side: a few palm trees, clustered together. It must mean a spring or a well!

You spot a well amongst the trees. You're heading straight for it when something alarming happens: you sink straight down into the ground!

Quicksand! Thinking fast, you throw your blanket away onto solid ground. It's cold in the quicksand, and you'll need it when you get out . . . if you get out. The quicksand's up to your waist now. Should you risk trying to throw your heavy backpack to the safety of solid ground? You could lose everything if it falls in.

If you decide to keep your backpack on, go to page 78.

If you decide to throw it to the side, go to page 86.

There's plenty of water for you to drink in the well, though there's nothing for you to eat. Luckily, you have enough sachets of salt in your backpack to ensure that you don't get hyponatraemia (see page 25).

You exist for weeks, sheltering from the sun during the day and exercising at night to keep warm – making sure you don't stray too far and get lost. You've started talking to yourself. At first you're tempted to try and kill a lizard or a jerboa to eat, but they're too fast for you. After a while you stop feeling hungry anyway, and you start talking to the lizards instead. They don't reply.

After several weeks alone in the desert, you start to feel very weak from lack of food. One day you spot a camel train heading for the well. You can hardly believe it – in fact, you assume you're hallucinating. But it's real. This is a regular stop for the nomadic people on the camels, on their trading journey to replenish their water supplies. They get a big surprise when they discover you at the well.

The people help tend to your sunburn (you ran out of sun cream a while ago), offer you a small amount of food (too much would be bad for you), and take you with them to safety. You're safe at last, but you can't help wondering that things might have been a bit more interesting if you'd set off into the desert instead. Or would it . . .

The end.

You stumble along the sand dune, sweating even though the night is cold. You're sure this is the right way, so you're determined to keep going. Your boots are filled with sand, and you keep sinking into the sand as you stumble and slip down the dune. Your progress is painfully slow.

Eventually, you realise that you can't carry on — but by this time it's too late. You're in the middle of a sea of undulating sand, and your water is very low. Without any means of finding more water, you die.

The end.

Sand Dunes

- The sand dunes of the Sahara (called ergs, or sand seas) stretch for hundreds of kilometres and can be more than 180 metres high.

- The Saharan winds have rubbed the sand into tiny grains, so the sand is very fine, and therefore very difficult to cross. Travellers avoid the Great Western and Great Eastern Ergs, between Beni Abbes in Algeria and Ghadamis in Libya.

- The Great Western and Great Eastern Ergs cover most of Algeria, the Selima Erg covers more than 4,500 square kilometres in Libya, and the Erg Cherch stretches for nearly 1000 kilometres across Mali and Algeria.

- Ergs are formed by winds sweeping sand into heaps. Some dunes have a gentle slope on the windward side, with a steep drop on the side opposite the wind. Seif dunes are parallel to the prevailing winds and have sharp ridge lines.

- During sandstorms, great quantities of sand can be moved, completely altering the landscape.

You find out fairly quickly that it isn't a good idea to get close to ostriches. They are big, can be aggressive, and have very sharp claws on their feet that can kill a human being. Added to this, they can run very fast – 70 kilometres per hour – so you definitely won't be able to outrun them.

These ostriches have young with them, so they're especially jumpy. A couple of the bigger birds trot away from the others towards you, watching you with what you imagine is an evil glint in their eyes. You remember hearing that birds like these can be tricked into thinking you're bigger than you are if you raise your arms over your head. You raise your arms, but this seems to be the last straw for one of the ostriches, which sprints towards you.

The giant bird attacks by kicking out with its feet, which are armed with long, sharp claws. With one blow, you are dead.

The end.

Ostriches

- Ostriches are the largest birds on the planet – up to 2.7 metres tall and 160 kilograms in weight.

- They live in African savannahs and deserts, though they rarely stray into the Sahara Desert.

- Ostriches don't need to drink – they can get all the water they need from the plants they eat. They also eat insects and lizards.

- The birds can sprint up to 70 kilometres per hour, and keep up a speed of 50 kilometres per hour over distances, covering up to five metres in just one stride.

- Ostriches live in small herds of about ten birds. Their giant eggs weigh as much as 24 chicken eggs!

- These huge birds defend themselves from lions with their long claws – so it's not surprising that they are dangerous to humans, and kill a small number of people every year (usually on ostrich farms). Like many animals, they're especially prone to aggression when they have young to defend.

You cut open the fruit with your knife. Inside there's greenish-white pulp and dark seeds. It looks quite appetising, and you tentatively take a small bite. Pah! You spit the pulp and seeds out quickly – it tastes awful! The bitter taste makes you thirsty. You take a swig from your water bottle and spit it out before drinking some, in case the fruit is poisonous.

In fact it's a desert gourd, which isn't poisonous, just foul-tasting. But you were taking a big chance by eating a fruit when you didn't know what it was. What were you thinking? You've had a lucky escape.

You decide to look for another water source.

Go to page 72.

Desert Gourd

- The desert gourd is a member of the watermelon family. It produces a vine that creeps across the desert floor, each one up to three metres long. It has round fruits the size of an orange, which are yellow when ripe.

- The plant is quite common in the Sahara, as well as in desert-like conditions in many Arab countries, coastal India, and parts of the Mediterranean. It will grow in the hottest climates.

- Although the pulp is bitter and shouldn't be eaten, the succulent stems of the wild desert gourd can be used as an emergency water source – they can be chewed for their moisture.

- The seeds of the fruit are also edible – they're best roasted – and are rich in oil. The flowers can be eaten too.

You start digging your hole for the solar still with your trowel. The ground is hard, so it's tough work. You need to drink several times while you're digging. You hope that the water produced by the still is going to be enough. You wait all day, sheltering from the intense desert heat, while the still produces some fresh drinking water.

Unfortunately, it doesn't produce very much water at all – less than half a litre. It's not enough to keep you going. You're already dehydrated when you set off again at dusk. You don't find another water source in time to save you.

The end.

Making a Solar Still

- Dig a hole in the ground about 90 centimetres across and 45 centimetres deep. If you can find any, put some green leaves and grasses in the hole.

- Put your container in the centre of the hole, then cover the hole with a sheet of plastic, weighted down with a stone in the centre above the container.

- Anchor your plastic in place with sand or rocks.

- As the sun heats the air inside the hole, water vapour is produced, which condenses on the plastic and runs down into the container. Green plants will help make more water vapour.

- You can also use a solar still to distil pure water from undrinkable water, such as sea water – put the contaminated water in a larger container at the bottom of the hole, with a collecting can in the middle as before.

- Beware: a solar still can also act as a trap for snakes and creepy crawlies, which might be able to get in but not get out again.

You need water to replenish your supplies. You know how to make a solar still – though that would mean setting it up and then waiting during the day. Or you could just keep walking and hope that you find another water source.

If you decide to make a solar still, go to page 70.

If you decide to look for another water source go to page 52.

You hate retracing your steps, but you think it's important to wash the wound, which is painful and angry looking. You're grateful for the bright moonlight as you find the well again and draw up some water to wash your wound. You even find a forgotten tube of antiseptic cream at the bottom of your backpack.

As you set off again, keeping well away from any animals you spot, you notice that there are a few clouds in the sky. The moon's still shining, but every so often a cloud moves in front of it, making it very difficult to see where you're going.

Go to page 84.

You slow down to a walk. You're sure this was the right thing to do – sweating makes your body lose salt as well as water, and not enough of either can result in death. You're not sure where you're going anyway, so getting there fast isn't going to make much difference.

There are some strange barking and whooping noises coming from high ground to your right. You think it sounds a bit like chimpanzees, though you know that chimps don't live here. As you walk, the sounds get louder – and some of it sounds like laughter! Suddenly you spot them, dark shapes amongst the rock. It's a group of hyenas. What should you do?

If you decide to run away and hide, go to page 60.

If you decide to walk confidently past them, go to page 40.

The wind is stronger now. It grabs your scarf and almost whisks it away. You wrap it around your mouth and nose in the sandy air, and have to put up your hands to shield your eyes. It's difficult to see anyway, because the moon is behind clouds.

The wind is howling now, the sand begins to whirl, and soon you can hardly see anything at all. The sandstorm is getting worse. You have to shelter somewhere fast.

If you decide to shelter behind some large rocks on higher ground, go to page 87.

If you decide to shelter beside a nearby dune, on lower ground, go to page 42.

You jump down into the wadi bottom and walk along the dry stream bed, which is rapidly turning to mud as the rain becomes heavier. You start to become alarmed at how quickly the thirsty ground has become thick, cloying mud . . . and you realise that this is a bad place to walk in a heavy downpour. You need to get out of the water and into some kind of shelter – fast!

You make for the side of the wadi . . . but as you do so there's a roaring sound, and suddenly a huge torrent of water comes rushing around a bend in the dry river bed, sweeping you off your feet like a tsunami. Every time you come up for air, spluttering, the swirling water drags you down again. Half-drowned, you are bashed against a large rock.

The end.

Flash Floods

You might not have thought you'd end up being swept away by a flood in the middle of a desert, but flash floods are one of the greatest perils of deserts around the world . . .

- Storms in deserts don't happen very often, but when they do they can release a huge amount of rain very quickly.

- Flash floods can happen without warning. The storm that feeds the flood could be miles away.

- Be especially careful in canyons, which can channel water like a giant water hose.

- In the US, on average, flash floods are responsible for more deaths than hurricanes each year.

You struggle in the horrible, cloying quicksand but it only makes you sink further. The backpack is heavy and the bottom of it is already getting wet. You're very cold, wet, and now you're starting to really panic.

Then you have an idea: what if you spread your weight more evenly across the surface? You lean to the side and bring your legs up. You reach out towards the edge of the quicksand – you can now see the difference in colour of the dry ground – all the while trying to keep the backpack out of the sand as much as possible. You're floating! It's quite easy to move to the side, even with your heavy backpack weighing you down.

You haul yourself out of the quicksand, quickly fling off your wet clothes and wrap yourself in the blanket, jogging on the spot to keep warm. When you're fairly dry, you step carefully around the quicksand to get water from the well.

With your bottles full of precious water, you set off. A cloud scuds across the moon, dimming your view of the desert. Then another. The wind starts to pick up – you can hear it howling as it scours the dry earth.

Go to page 75.

Quicksand

It would have been a better idea to have taken off your heavy backpack, but quicksand isn't as dangerous as you might have thought.

- Quicksand is simply very wet sand, clay or silt. It can't suck you down (despite the myths about bottomless pits of doom).

- It looks just like ordinary sand, apart from the difference in colour if the surrounding sand is dry, so it's easy to wander into it by accident.

- It's quite rare for quicksand to be deep enough that you can't reach the bottom.

- If you find yourself in quicksand, remove heavy objects and float across the surface to the side. Don't remain upright.

- Quicksand is usually made by underground springs pushing water upwards into sand or silt – here, it's the spring that feeds the well.

As you lick your parched lips, you realise that you should have slowed down well before now. In the desert, your main priority should be making sure you have enough water for the amount of work you're doing. You die of dehydration after a few days.

The end.

Keeping Hydrated

- If you live in a temperate climate, you will probably be surprised at how quickly you can become dehydrated in a desert. Check the chart on page 119 to work out how much water you need.

- If you're lost in the desert, don't walk during the day because you don't know where your next water source might be.

- Don't run at any time, unless you absolutely have to (for example, if you're being pursued by an angry baboon).

- We lose most water from sweating. If you're very hot and suddenly stop sweating, you have heat stroke and need medical attention immediately.

- During the Second World War, the US army had a theory that soldiers could be trained to make do with less water, by gradually reducing their water supplies each day. It didn't work and caused hundreds of sick, dehydrated soldiers.

- Don't eat, because water is used up digesting food – you need it for cooling you down more than you need the food.

- Don't rely on thirst as a guide to your water requirements. Remember that the early stages of dehydration don't have any symptoms, and even mild dehydration can limit how well your body works.

- Dehydration also reduces concentration and alertness, which you're probably going to need in a survival situation.

- If your pee is dark in colour, you're already dehydrated and need to drink.

You head for the rocks in the half-light. As you climb them, the sun starts to sink over the horizon and the sky darkens even more.

You decide to climb as high as you can to get a good view before the light goes completely . . . however, this close to the equator, there isn't much of a twilight – darkness falls quickly, taking you by surprise. You've made a big mistake in climbing up here, especially without any kind of climbing gear or safety equipment.

You didn't really think this one through, did you? You get a fantastic view of the setting sun, but as darkness descends you slip on some loose rocks and fall to your death. Look on the bright side: at least your last memory is of a beautiful sunset.

The end.

You find some rocks that look as though they might be a good place to rest during the day. You have a look around, trying to work out the best place to lay your blanket, where it will be shielded from the sun, when suddenly you are faced with one of the most hideous looking creatures you have ever seen . . .

It looks like some sort of weird spider, hairy and about ten centimetres long, with a huge head and hideous, over-sized jaws. Surely something this horrible has got to be venomous? It scuttles away from you at a surprising speed – faster than any spider – making you shudder.

If you decide to stay at these rocks, but keep away from the nasty-looking creature, which is obviously afraid of you, go to page 100.

If you decide to run away and find somewhere else to rest for the day, go to page 113.

The moon slips behind a cloud. You feel that there's a change in the air – the cold night feels slightly warmer. You sniff the air, and there is a dampness to it. Surely it's not going to rain in the Sahara Desert? If it is, then maybe finding water wasn't such a necessity after all.

The first fat drops of rain begin to fall. There's a wadi not far away, which looks nice and flat and easy to walk along. Or should you walk along the lower slopes of a mountainside to your right?

If you decide to walk along the high ground, go to page 88.

If you decide to walk along the wadi, go to page 76.

Rain in the Desert

- You might have thought that the whole point about deserts is the lack of rain. It is true that a desert is defined by its low annual rainfall, less than 250 millimetres. But deserts do get some rain – even in the Sahara.

- 'Average' rainfall isn't very useful if you want to know whether or not it's likely to rain in a desert, because the amount of rainfall is so erratic from year to year. One year an area might have 400 millimetres of rainfall, 300 millimetres the next, and none at all the following year. The average is still below 250 millimetres.

- The low rainfall means that plants and animals have had to adapt to the arid conditions (see page 27). The resurrection plant is one of the most incredible. When it's dry, it blows about the desert like tumbleweed, brown and desiccated and dead-looking. But if it finds water it quickly absorbs it and unfurls its leaves. Then it waits for rain to fall. If it does, its seeds fall, germinate and produce shoots on the wet ground in a matter of hours. The plant can remain in its dried out state for a hundred years, and still come back to life when it finds water.

Y ou wriggle out of the backpack and fling it to the side. It slips on the edge, and gradually falls back into the quicksand. It's floating on the surface, but you can see it's starting to sink. Oh no! With a great squelch, you lunge for it – and to your surprise you discover that you can float on the quicksand. You reach the backpack, push it up onto solid ground, then clamber out yourself.

You're cold and wet, so you dry yourself as best you can with your blanket. Taking care not to fall into the quicksand again, you get water from the well. Quicksand isn't the swamp of deadly peril you'd imagined (see the information on page 79).

Clouds are racing across the sky, dimming the light of the moon. The wind has started to pick up.

Go to page 75.

You shelter behind a large rock, your scarf over your face to protect your eyes, nose and mouth. Sand whirls into the air in a choking cloud as the wind howls around you. All you can do is sit and wait with your eyes closed. Thankfully, it soon begins to die down. After half an hour, the storm has blown over. You get up and carry on walking, returning to flatter ground.

Suddenly you hear a loud barking sound – and then a shriek. A rain of loose stones descends from high rocks above you. Your heart pounding, you look up into the rocky hillside.

The moonlight reveals several big monkeys. Altogether you count twenty of them, and there might be more hiding in the rocks. A few of them are walking purposefully towards you. They have large, long, dog-like snouts. One of the bigger ones opens its mouth to reveal huge canine teeth. Maybe it's warning you off? Then again, they're only monkeys – how dangerous can they be?

If you decide to keep going past the baboons go to page 90.

If you decide to back off and go a different way, avoiding them, go to page 104.

The rain gets heavier quickly, drenching you. Soon it's a torrential downpour. It's difficult to see where you're going in the driving rain with the clouds hiding the moon, so you shelter by some rocks, amazed that you could be this cold and wet in the Sahara desert.

After a while, the rain stops. The sky clears and you can now see where you're going. The rocks drip, and so do you. You pick up your pace to keep warm. As you hurry along, you look down to the wadi and see that it's completely flooded – it's just as well you didn't take that route.

Go to page 98.

You're glad to have removed that horrible creature. There's a small spot where it had buried into your skin, and you wash it with some of your water, just to be on the safe side.

As you walk on you keep your eyes open for a new source of water to replenish your supplies.

Go to page 72.

As you pass closer to the baboon troop they call to one another (or maybe to you), making loud, scary-sounding noises – shrieks, screams and barks. A few of them run towards you, then sit staring at you.

You're becoming more and more nervous. You pick up a large rock and chuck it at one of the baboons – that should scare them off.

It doesn't. Instead, the baboons return fire with rocks of their own, several of which hit you. You realise, too late, that the best thing to do around potentially dangerous wild animals is to remain calm and back off. Unfortunately, one of the largest male baboons attacks you. There are baby baboons about and he sees you as a threat to the troop, particularly since you aimed that rock at one of them.

The end.

Baboons

- There are five species of baboon, all native to Africa and Arabia. They are some of the largest monkeys in the world, with the biggest males up to 37 kilograms, and up to about a metre tall.

- Baboons will eat almost anything: fruit, grass, seeds and roots, but also meat – rodents and birds, and even the young of large mammals.

- Baboons form large groups called troops – there might be hundreds in a very large one.

- They communicate with one another using a variety of different calls with different meanings.

- Baboons can be aggressive and have been known to hurt human beings – but you were very unlucky to be killed.

It's not dark yet, but the sun is beginning to sink and the temperature has dropped, so you decide to get up and get moving.

You could take higher ground, up some quite steep rocks, to get a good view of your surroundings. Or you could carry on along the stone covered, flat ground.

If you decide to take the higher ground, go to page 82.

If you decide to walk along the flatter ground, go to page 109.

As you get closer, you can see that the creatures are definitely ostriches. There are ten of them, you think. They're probably only about a hundred metres or so away from you.

You are pretty sure that ostriches are never far from water. Should you approach them and find their water source? Or do you worry that the ostriches could be dangerous?

If you decide to get closer to the ostriches, go to page 66.

If you decide to find water somewhere else, go to page 105.

You walk towards the shimmering water, but it doesn't seem to be getting any closer. After an hour or so of walking, you're so hot that your water supplies are dangerously low. You hope you get to the sparkling lake soon.

Unfortunately, you don't, because there's no water there at all – it's an effect of the hot sun on the desert sand. After a while, you're out of water and can't find any means of finding more.

The end.

Mirages

- Sometimes the heat of the desert will produce a layer of cooler air lying on top of a much hotter layer (or the other way around). Sunlight is refracted (bent) differently, resulting in an optical illusion: two images appear. An area of sky might be repeated below it on the desert sand, resembling a lake.

- A patch of sky repeated on the desert floor is an 'inferior mirage', because it's underneath the true image. Some mirages are 'superior', where the second image appears above the true one – so you might see a camel in mid-air above a camel on the ground.

- Mirages aren't hallucinations brought on by extreme thirst, as they're sometimes portrayed. They are optical illusions and can be captured on camera.

You set off after the camels in the breaking dawn – but they're too quick for you. Before long they are too far away for you to bother chasing them any more.

It's getting light – soon it will be hot. Should you find somewhere to rest for the day, or carry on – at least for a while – and hope that you find rescue soon?

If you decide to rest, go to page 83.

If you decide to keep going, go to page 112.

Camels

- A Bactrian (or Asian) camel has two humps, while a dromedary (or Arabian camel) has one. The humps don't store water, they contain fat. By keeping most of their fat in one place, camels can keep cooler. If you see a camel with a very floppy hump, it's probably a hungry camel.

- Camels spit when they're angry. They have four separate chambers to their stomachs and can regurgitate undigested food. They often spit it at whatever is bothering them.

- Camels are specially adapted to desert conditions:

  » They have extra long, curly eyelashes to keep sand out, and an extra eyelid to wipe it away.

  » They don't pant and hardly sweat; the moisture they breathe out is recycled because it trickles down a groove below their nostril and back into their mouth. They can also close their nostrils between breaths to keep out sand.

  » They have large soft pads on their feet that are specially adapted for travelling on sand.

  » They hardly lose any water in their poo. When it's fresh, it's already dry enough to burn on a fire (and people do use camel dung as fuel).

- All these adaptations mean that a camel can travel 160 kilometres in the desert without water. When it does find water to drink, a camel might drink 135 litres of water in less than 15 minutes.

A cascade of pebbles skitters down the rocks in front of you. You look up: there's a group of seven or eight sheep or goats up there. They have big, curled horns, manes and hairy legs. They are staring at you in the moonlight. Although they're quite big animals, each of them looks as though it's precariously balanced on the side of the cliff.

You suppose that these animals must have some access to water and it clearly looks as though they live on this mountain. If you climbed up after them, maybe you'd find pools of water among the higher rocks? If so, this could be a good place to make a camp and wait to be rescued.

If you decide to climb up the mountain after the animals, go to page 106

If you decide to keep walking along the lower slopes, ignoring the sheep, go to page 110.

It's already really hot now, and you realise that it's going to get hotter as the sun climbs higher in the sky. In the distance, to the east, shimmers a wide stretch of blue. Could it be water sparkling in the sun? Maybe it's an oasis?

If you decide to go and investigate, go to page 94.

If you decide to keep going the way you're heading, go to page 103.

You lay your blanket down in a spot that will be shaded when the sun comes up, and sit down to take a drink. You reach for your backpack and just as you're about to put your hand on the fastener, the hideous looking spider creature scuttles across it! You jerk your hand back and lurch away from it, letting out a little scream.

Shivering with revulsion, you decide that there must be a number of these creatures here, and those jaws could probably give you a very nasty bite, whether they're venomous or not. You decide to make your bed for the day somewhere else.

Go to page 113.

Solpugids

- Although these creatures are sometimes called camel spiders, sun spiders or wind spiders, they're not true spiders at all. They're actually solpugids, which are arachnids, like spiders and scorpions, but they're not quite the same as either creature.

- They have a huge head and jaws – in fact they have the biggest jaws in relation to their size of any creature on Earth.

- There are lots of myths came about solpugids, probably because they are so horrible to look at. Some of these myths are that they chase people and can run at incredible speeds (they do run very fast, up to 16 kilometres per hour, but not faster than you!); they eat people (and camels) alive while they're asleep; they have extremely powerful venom. Thankfully, none of them is true, and in fact they're not venomous.

- Camel spiders are about 15 centimetres long (though there are rumours that they're much bigger).

You start digging at the outside bend of the dry stream bed. The ground is hard and you start to sweat – you're very glad that it's not too hot yet, though it's getting hotter all the time as the sun climbs higher.

You haven't dug very deep when your spade makes a squelching noise. Thank goodness! You dig deeper and the hole fills with water. You rest in the shade of a boulder and boil the water (just to be on the safe side), then fill your bottles.

It won't be long before it's too hot to continue walking.

Go to page 99.

Y ou're getting very hot and decide to stop and rest for the day. There's some high ground to one side of you, which you've been following for a while, where there are plenty of big rocks to offer shade. You make yourself comfortable and wait out the rest of the hot day, wondering if you're ever going to get out of the desert alive.

At long last, the sun starts to sink. You gather up your blanket and belongings and start walking. The rocks where you've been sheltering slope down to ground level just ahead of you. On the other side of them, you notice a flash of green. It looks as though there are some trees on the other side of the rocks — and what look like buildings, too. Maybe you've been waiting the whole day only an hour's walk from an oasis!

Go to page 114.

You carefully back off, glancing up every now and again at the monkeys, mindful not to make eye contact in case they see it as a threat. One of the males comes further towards you, then sits on a rock, staring.

You were right to be wary of the monkeys – they are baboons, which can sometimes be dangerous to people.

When you're 50 metres or so away from them, you start to relax.

Go to page 84.

You need some water, but, since there's no obvious water source around, you'll need to dig. Now's the time to do it, before it gets really hot – if you leave it till later, you might end up becoming dehydrated before you've found enough water.

You can see some greenery in the distance – it could be some sort of tree. You can also make out a dry stream bed in the opposite direction. Where should you choose to dig?

If you decide to dig at the tree, go to page 111.

If you decide to dig at the stream, go to page 102.

The sheep – or goats, it's difficult to tell – are facing your way, munching the scraggly grass and leaves that grow on the mountainside. It's going to be a bit tricky, but the moon is bright, and you're confident of your climbing abilities.

You clamber up the rocks to a small ledge. As you straighten up, the animals above you suddenly turn and run off up the mountain, skittering across the rocks so fast you can hardly tell which way they went. Unfortunately, they've dislodged several large rocks, which bounce down the mountainside, knocking you off your feet and to your death.

The end.

Barbary Sheep

- Barbary sheep are sandy coloured, with a mane and hairy legs. They weigh up to 145 kilograms, and measure up to about one metre tall.

- They live in mountainous areas, and are extremely agile at moving about on steep rocks – they can jump up to two metres high from a standing start. In their mountain environment, they're safe from predators.

- Barbary sheep are mostly crepuscular, which means they are active at dawn and dusk. They do this to avoid the heat of the day.

- They get all their moisture from the plants they eat, and don't need to drink at all. But if there's water available they'll drink and wallow in it.

- Barbary sheep aren't aggressive, and run away at the first sign of danger.

You're pretty sure that following those camels would have been pointless – after all, they're much better equipped for moving in the desert than you are, and much faster too.

The sky is lightening. As you walk, the sun comes up. The desert looks beautiful bathed in the dawn light. But it can be deadly too. You wonder how long it will be before you find an oasis and people to help you. Or whether you ever will.

You decide to look on the bright side: you're feeling OK, and you have plenty of water. So you decide to keep walking, at least for a while, until the heat becomes too intense.

Go to page 99.

The light's fading, and you know it won't be long until it's gone completely. You hope for another bright, moonlit night.

From the corner of your eye, you spot a movement. Far in the distance, just emerging from behind a low hill, there's a camel. Squinting at it, you think you can make out the outline of a person riding it. Behind the camel there's another one – and another one following that. They're walking in a line, one behind the other. It must be a camel train!

You call out, as loudly as you can. But even to you, your voice sounds feeble. You know it won't reach the camel riders. Still, you hope, maybe they're not far away from their destination – perhaps they're late getting back.

You hurry onwards, following the direction of the camels.

Go to page 114.

You haven't gone far when you spot a different kind of creature in the distance: camels.

They're a few hundred metres or so away, loping along the barren ground. Sadly, there aren't any people with them.

Still, maybe you should follow them – you guess they'll eventually lead you to water?

If you decide to follow the camels, go to page 96.

If you decide not to, go to page 108.

As you get closer, you see that it's a single tree, four or five metres high, standing alone in parched-looking soil. It has small, green leaves, and it's covered in long, vicious looking spines. But you're not interested in eating its leaves or climbing it – just in the water it must be drinking.

In fact the tree is an acacia tree, also known as a thorn tree. Its sharp thorns protect it from grazing animals. An acacia's roots can extend many metres underground in order to find water to sustain it.

You start to dig in the hard, parched earth. With every spade of soil you hope to see water trickling into the hole, but the earth is dry.

You're sweating a lot, and you've drunk the last of your water. You've no choice but to carry on digging. Soon you're completely exhausted and dehydrated. With no other source of water and no energy to carry on digging you soon die.

The end.

The sun isn't yet over the horizon, and it's still cool. You walk steadily, without any idea of where you're heading. You hope you'll spot something that might help you find other people soon.

Suddenly you do spot something: a movement by some rocks in the distance. In the half-light you can't work out what it is. Maybe animals . . . maybe people.

If you decide to go and investigate, go to page 93.

If you decide not to, go to page 105.

You don't have to go far to find some more large rocks to give you shelter from the sun. You carry out a careful inspection to make sure there aren't any more creatures like that revolting thing you just saw (it was a solpugid – see page 101). After a thorough investigation, you're satisfied that there aren't, and you can't see any snakes, scorpions or other creepy crawlies either.

You spread your blanket on the floor and put your backpack down. Before you lie down you have an idea: you gather a big pile of stones and spell out SOS in huge letters on the desert floor. You never know, a passing helicopter might spot them. You finish just as the sun starts to go down.

Go to page 92.

The lights of an oasis twinkle in the darkness. Palm trees sway in a gentle breeze. It's the most welcome sight you've ever seen.

You're almost crying with relief as you get closer. You call out, and two people come running. They offer shelter, food and water, and promise to get you back to your friends and family the next day.

Soon you're home. You've survived your amazing Saharan adventure.

The end.

Oases

- An oasis is a fertile area in a desert, fed by a source of fresh water. It might be just a few palm trees around a well, or much bigger. For example, the Kharga Oasis in Egypt is 160 kilometres long, and has a population of more than 100,000.

- Underground water sources called aquifers supply most oases. The water might come up to the surface naturally, in an underground spring, or people might dig wells to get to the aquifer.

- Palms are planted all around oases to keep out the desert sands. People also plant crops, such as dates (which grow on certain types of palm tree), olives, figs, oranges, lemons, and cotton.

- The Nile River is the only permanent river in the Sahara. The rest of the region's water lies in underground aquifers.

- There are about 90 major oases in the Sahara, but travelling between them might take days.

The People of the Sahara Desert

People are totally dependent on water, so permanent homes in the Sahara are limited to oases, and the towns and cities on the desert fringes. But some people who live in the Sahara don't have permanent homes: nomads spend some of the year travelling through the desert and the rest in the mountains or at an oasis.

Nomads live by herding camels, sheep and goats and trading between oases and cities on the edge of the desert. Salt is important for trade because it's in short supply in the Sahara, so for hundreds of years the Tuareg nomads have transported it on camel trains. In Niger they still do – the Tuareg cross the desert to the Bilma oasis, then transport it, packed into cakes or cone shapes, for trade elsewhere. In the past they traded in gold and spices too. Today, there are around a million Tuareg people in and around the Sahara – some of them still lead a nomadic lifestyle, while others have settled in towns and cities.

Sahara Mountains

There are several mountain ranges within the Sahara Desert. The Air Mountains in northern Niger rise to more than 1,800 metres and cover more than 82,000 square kilometres. Mount Emi Koussi, in the Tibesti Mountains of northern Chad, is the highest peak in the Sahara at 3,415 metres high. The Tassili n'Ajjer mountain range in Algeria covers 72,000 square kilometres and is famous for its prehistoric rock art, which reveals that the Sahara once had a very different climate: hippos and crocodiles lived here during the Stone Age.

Expanding Sahara

The Sahel borders the Sahara Desert to the south. Changing patterns of rainfall, clearing land for fuel, and intensive farming have led to the spread of the desert. Areas that were once green and forested are now dry and lifeless.

Other Deserts

Deserts are places where there is very little rainfall. While all of them are dry, not all of them are hot. The Antarctic is the largest desert in the world, more than half as big again as the Sahara. It receives an average of 200 millimetres of rainfall per year in its coastal regions, less inland. It's the coldest place on earth: the temperature plummets to as low as -89 degrees Celsius.

Deserts take up around a third of the Earth's land surface. Other deserts around the world include . . .

- The Gobi Desert stretches for nearly 1.3 million square kilometres across China and Mongolia. It's a cold desert, though temperatures in some areas can reach 35 degrees Celsius. Like the Sahara, it has vast sand dunes, but most of the Gobi Desert is bare rock.

- The Atacama Desert in Chile is high above sea level, and the driest place on earth after Antarctica. In some parts of the desert rainfall has never been recorded, and there the desert is completely barren.

- The Mojave Desert in North America spans California, Nevada and Utah. It includes one of the most famously hot and inhospitable places on earth, Death Valley, where the temperature can reach 54 degrees Celsius in summer.

- The Namib Desert in southern Africa stretches for 2,000 kilometres along the coasts of Angola, Namibia and South Africa. It has vast sand dunes near the coast – the largest are 300 metres high and 30 kilometres long.

How much water do you need to drink?

Hard work in sun •••••••
Moderate work in sun – – – – –
Rest in shade ————

Daily water requirement in litres

Air temperature in degrees C

The instructions on this water chart are merely a guide. You will need too seek professional help for a more accurate chart.

Real-life Lost in the Desert Stories

People really have ended up lost in the Sahara Desert. Not all of them have lived to tell the tale.

The Marathon des Sables (Marathon of the Sands) is an extreme 254-kilometre marathon run across the Sahara Desert in Morocco over six days. It's a gruelling race, considered the most difficult foot race in the world. Mauro Prosperi, an Italian policeman, was competing in the 1994 Marathon des Sables, when a sandstorm blew up. In the swirling sand, he was unable to see and became completely lost. Mauro didn't have any water on him at all, and yet he survived for nine days. He drank his own urine (which is absolutely NOT recommended!), and ate snakes, scorpions, lizards, and some bats that he discovered while sheltering in an abandoned Muslim shrine. He wasn't lucky enough to come across any wells or water holes, so it's incredible that he survived. Eventually, he met a nomad family, who helped him and returned him to safety. He had walked 200 kilometres away from the course of the marathon. Mauro made a complete recovery and, surprisingly, he has since completed the Marathon des Sables many times.

According to Ancient Greek historian Heroditas, an entire Persian army got lost in the Sahara Desert and never found their way out. In 525 BC the 50,000-strong army was sent into the Sahara by Persian King Cambyses II. Halfway across the desert, heading for the remote Siwa Oasis in Egypt, an immense sandstorm blew up. Not one of the men ever made it to the oasis. People have been looking for them, or their remains, ever since.

Glossary

adobe a natural building material made from sand, clay and water

amoebae small organisms made of only one cell

antibiotics drugs that kill bacteria

aquifer an underground water source

arid dry, lacking a water source

carrion dead animals

contaminated unclean

crepuscular active at dawn and dusk

disoriented confused, lost

dysentery an infection causing diarrhoea

epidemics diseases affecting large numbers of people at once

ergs sand dunes

escarpment a steep slope or cliff

flash flood sudden, quick flooding caused by very heavy rain

germinate begin to grow and develop

hallucinations things you can see that do not really exist

hamadas desert landscapes consisting of high, exposed rock

hemisphere half of the Earth

hyponatraemia a lack of salt in the blood

metabolic rate the amount of energy used

mirage an optical illusion caused by light rays bending to produce an image such as water

nomads people who do not have one permanent home but move from one place to another

oases isolated areas of vegetation in deserts

parasite a creature that lives by feeding on another creature

plains broad expanses of flat land

proximity how close something is

refracted light or other waves being bent

regs rocky plains

regurgitate bring swallowed food out of the mouth

scavengers creatures that feed on dead animals or plants

sepsis blood poisoning

serrated having a notched or saw-like edge

silt a grainy material that is a bit thicker than sand

succulent juicy, water-storing

tick a small parasite living on the blood of other creatures

venomous capable of injecting venom

wadis the Arabic word for dry river bed or valley

Index

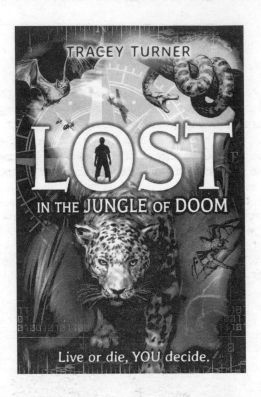

Lost... In the Jungle of Doom

You've survived the terrifying creatures and deadly dehydration of the Sahara Desert but can you make it through the dark and dangerous Amazon Rainforest in one piece? From ferocious jaguars to poisonous fruits, have you got with it takes to make it out alive?

With danger lurking behind every corner, will you be able to make it to safety and escape the deadly perils hiding in the shadowy depths?

Live or die – you decide.

£4.99   ISBN 9781408194652

Extract from Lost... In the Jungle of Doom

You look towards the spot where you thought you heard the sound. You still can't see anything. You decide to creep a bit further forward, taking care to be quiet, but twigs snap and leaves rustle as you move. You part the branches of a low-growing plant, peering into the greenish gloom of the rainforest at dawn . . .

You think you see a movement. There's something there! You look more closely at the spot and almost cry out in fear: a pair of yellow eyes is staring straight at you! You can make out the rest of the animal now – a huge cat, with spotted fur and a long tail. A jaguar. You gulp. The animal snarls, revealing long, pointed teeth. It looks as though it's about to pounce!

If you decide to run away, go to page 24.

If you decide to stand your ground, go to page 26.